# TEENAGE MUTANT NINJA TURTLES™

# FRIENDS TILL THE END!

adapted by Steve Murphy
based on the original teleplay
"Fallen Angel"
by Marty Isenberg
illustrated by Bob Ostrom

Simon Spotlight
New York    London    Toronto    Sydney

Based on the TV series *Teenage Mutant Ninja Turtles™*

as seen on Fox and Cartoon Network™.

SIMON SPOTLIGHT

An imprint of Simon & Schuster Children's Publishing Division

1230 Avenue of the Americas, New York, New York 10020

© 2004 Mirage Studios, Inc. *Teenage Mutant Ninja Turtles™*

is a trademark of Mirage Studios, Inc. All rights reserved.

SIMON SPOTLIGHT and colophon are registered trademarks of Simon & Schuster, Inc.

Manufactured in the United States of America

First Edition   10 9 8 7 6 5 4 3 2 1

ISBN 0-689-87006-X

"I remember the first time I saw you, Angel," said Raphael as he reached for another slice of pizza. "It was right after you helped the Purple Dragons rob that appliance store. You were waiting outside. I thought you looked pretty cool. Way too cool to be hanging out with a no-good group like the Purple Dragons."

Raphael and Angel had gathered with Casey Jones, Leonardo, Michelangelo, and Donatello to celebrate the one-year anniversary since the Turtles first met Angel.

"You were right, Raph," said Angel. I *was* too cool for the Purple Dragons, but I needed some help figuring that out."

"Hey, what are friends for!" said Leonardo.

Angel grinned. "I have to admit, though, that when I first got a good look at you and your brothers I thought you were all, well, pretty *funky* looking!"

"Yeah, well, that was a pretty funky night," said Casey. "It started off simple enough, with me and the boys catching the Dragons red-handed in the middle of ripping off that store."

"I remember Raphael asked the Dragons, 'Now, class, who can tell me what you've done wrong?'" continued Casey.

"And then I said, 'You mean besides being badly dressed, lawbreaking, good-for-nothing low-life street punks?'"

The group laughed.

"Like I said," continued Casey, "it was a simple enough matter that night. At least until I spotted Angel.

"She bugged out when she recognized me. She asked me why I was interfering. I remember looking her straight in the eye and saying: 'I'm trying to stop you from making the biggest mistake of your life.'

"Then Angel said something about the Dragons being like family and ran off."

"But I promised her Grandma that I'd look out for her. So I wasn't going to let her get away that easily. The next night I decided to keep an eye out on her apartment just in case some Purple Dragon punks showed up."

"Imagine my surprise when I saw Angel sneak out in the middle of the night! I was so mad that I wanted to jump out and yell at her, but I remembered Splinter telling me to always look before I leap. So instead I decided to follow her. And Angel led me right to the Purple Dragons's headquarters!"

"I followed Angel over to the fight ring," Casey said. "I knew she didn't stand a chance. I had to do something. So I did the one thing I know best."

"Casey was way outnumbered," said Angel, continuing the story, "plus that one guy was humongous—the one named Hun."

"'Tie Jones up,' Hun rumbled, with a voice like an avalanche. 'We'll play some more with him later,'" said Angel.

"Casey looked up at me and whispered, 'Go get my *real* friends.' Then he passed out. Of course he meant you guys—the funky bunch."

"It didn't take me long to find you guys. Actually you found me first, approaching me silently from the darkness like living shadows. I explained what had happened to Casey and how we had to save him from the Dragons. I remember *you* answering, Michelangelo. 'Of course, that's what friends are for,' you said. Simple as that."

"One of the first lessons Splinter taught us is that friends and family are supposed to be there for each other—at all times," said Leonardo. "It *is* that simple."

The Turtles looked at each other in agreement. Then Donatello started laughing.

"What's so funny?" asked Leonardo.

"I was just remembering what happened when Angel tried to get us to wear disguises before heading out after Casey," Donatello said.

"Remember?" asked Donatello. "We went through all that used clothing from April's antique store. It was like dressing up for Halloween!

"Then Angel intervened. She dressed us up and showed us how to act so we would fit in, and then hustled us over to the Purple Dragons's club."

"At the club," continued Donatello, "Leo and Raph entered the steel fight cage to keep Hun busy. Meanwhile Angel led Mike and me up to the club's overhead catwalks in order to free Casey, who was hanging upside down from the ceiling."

"From the catwalk Angel turned the spotlight directly into the eyes of Casey's guards. Then Mike and I could finish the job with perfectly timed flying drop-kicks."

"Casey barely had time to thank Angel when we heard what sounded like a ton of steel bars striking the cement floor. We looked down and saw that Hun had pulled down the steel cage that Leo and Raph had been in.

"Fortunately for us Hun wasn't very smart," said Donatello. "He had also pulled the cage down on top of himself!"

"I ran down from the catwalk just in time to see Casey standing over Hun about to hurt him. 'This one's for my father,' snarled Casey. But before Casey could do anything, Angel reached out to stop him.

"'Angel! What are you doing?' Casey yelled, as Angel pulled him away from Hun.

"'Stopping you from doing something you might regret,' replied Angel.

"Casey stared at her. 'You're right,' he said. 'Thanks.'

"'No problem,' she replied. 'That's what friends are for.'"

"Right," echoed Casey, "that *is* what friends are for!"